DISCOVER AND DO!

ANIMALS

GET HANDS-ON WITH SCIENCE

Written by Jane Lacey

W

FRANKLIN WATTS
LONDON • SYDNEY

Franklin Watts
First published in Great Britain in 2021
by The Watts Publishing Group
Copyright © The Watts Publishing Group, 2021

Produced for Franklin Watts by
White-Thomson Publishing Ltd
www.wtpub.co.uk

HB ISBN: 978 1 4451 7718 2
PB ISBN: 978 1 4451 7717 5

Editor: Katie Dicker
Series designer: Rocket Design (East Anglia) Ltd

Picture credits:
t=top b=bottom m=middle l=left r=right

Printed in China

Franklin Watts
An imprint of
Hachette Children's Group
Part of The Watts Publishing Group
Carmelite House
50 Victoria Embankment
London EC4Y 0DZ

An Hachette UK Company
www.hachettechildrens.co.uk

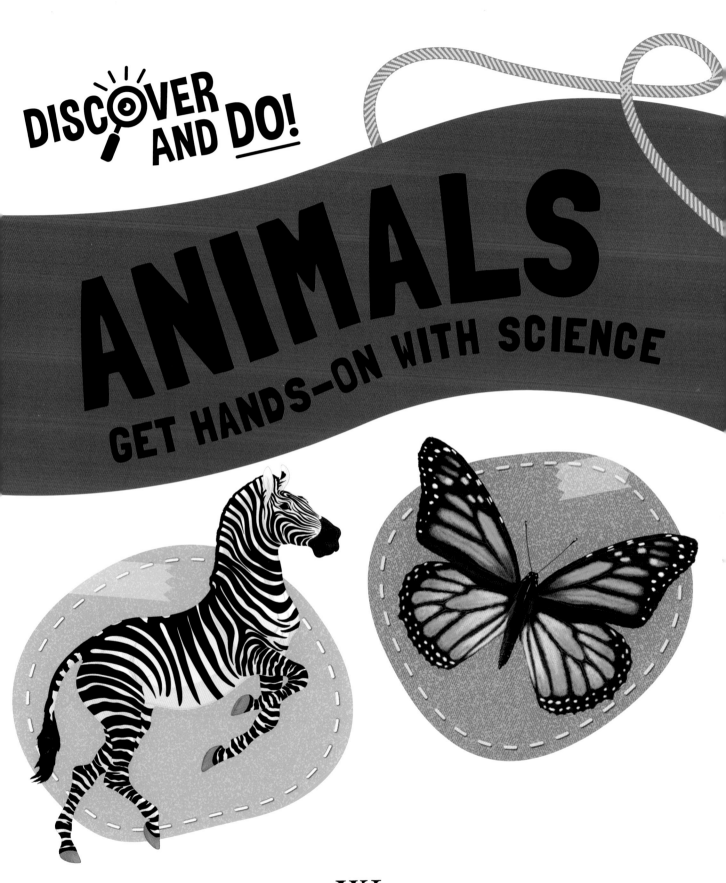

DISCOVER AND DO!

ANIMALS

GET HANDS-ON WITH SCIENCE

W
FRANKLIN WATTS
LONDON · SYDNEY

Contents

Words that appear in **bold** can be found in the glossary on pages 28–29.

WHAT ARE ANIMALS?

Animals are living things. About two million different types of animals, including humans, belong to the animal **kingdom**. We share our planet, Earth, with other animals so we need to care for them and their **habitats**.

Animal characteristics

Animals all have the same basic **characteristics**. They breathe in oxygen and breathe out carbon dioxide. They eat food and their bodies get rid of any waste. They move, sense the world around them, grow and **reproduce**. Animals do these things in different ways. For example, a bird moves by flying and breathes with its lungs. A fish swims and breathes through its **gills**.

Humans and fish are both animals, but humans cannot breathe naturally under water like fish.

Animal groups

Scientists have organised animals into groups. Each **species** of animal belongs to a group that shares similar characteristics. For example, the group called **mammals** includes humans, monkeys, elephants and mice. Some of the other main animal groups are fish, birds, insects, amphibians and reptiles.

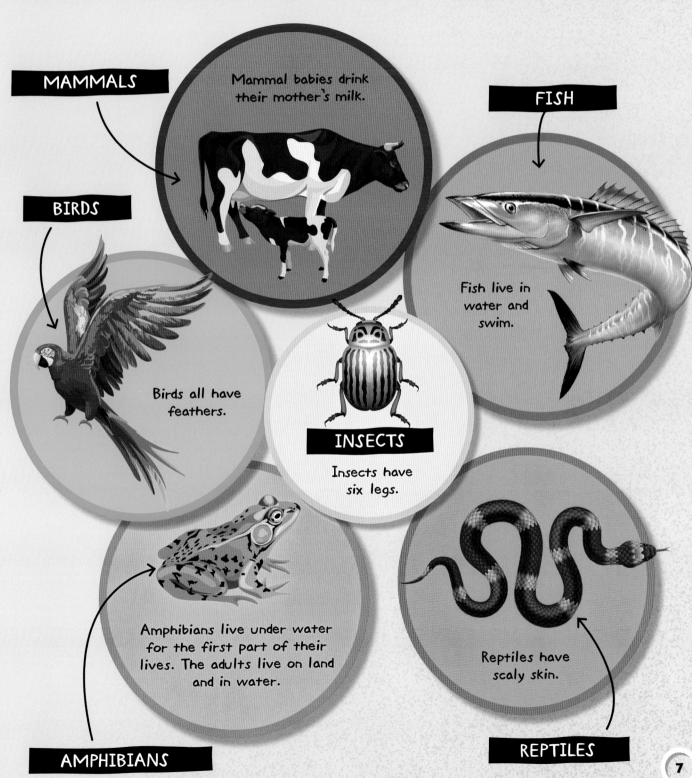

MAMMALS

Mammal babies drink their mother's milk.

FISH

Fish live in water and swim.

BIRDS

Birds all have feathers.

INSECTS

Insects have six legs.

AMPHIBIANS

Amphibians live under water for the first part of their lives. The adults live on land and in water.

REPTILES

Reptiles have scaly skin.

VERTEBRATES

All animal species can be divided into two main groups – animals with a backbone, called vertebrates, and animals without a backbone, called invertebrates. Mammals, fish, amphibians, reptiles and birds are all vertebrates.

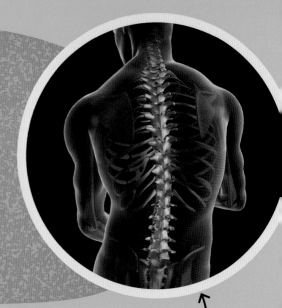

Your backbone supports you and lets you bend and move around.

Backbone

The backbone – also called the spine – is a row of small, knobbly bones joined together that supports the whole body. A crocodile's backbone runs from its head to its tail. A snake's backbone is very flexible and lets it coil and slither along the ground.

Crocodile

Skeleton

The bones of vertebrates are joined together to form a **skeleton** that gives their bodies a shape. Skeletons are hidden under the skin. You could probably guess what animal a skeleton belonged to by looking at its shape and size.

The shape of this horse matches the shape of its skeleton.

MAKE A MOVEABLE CROCODILE SKELETON

Ask an adult to help you with this activity

You will need:
- **sheet of A3 white card**
- **pencil**
- **black pen**
- **scissors**
- **pin**
- **6 paper fasteners**

1 On the white sheet of card, draw the templates shown below of the two parts of the crocodile skull, the body, the tail, the two front and two back legs, and the two back feet. Fill in the dark shapes with a black pen.

2 Cut out the templates.

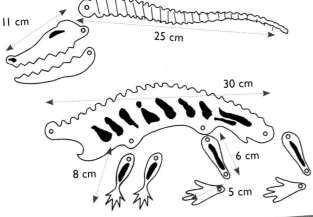

3 Ask an adult to use the pin to make small holes where the circles are marked. Push a paper fastener through the pin holes to make them bigger.

Fold back and forth along the lines of the tail, as if you were making a fan, to make it moveable.

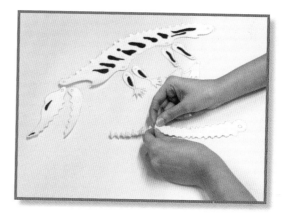

4 Join the skeleton parts together with paper fasteners where marked. Make sure each joint is loose enough for the parts to move. Watch the bones of your crocodile move as you walk it along!

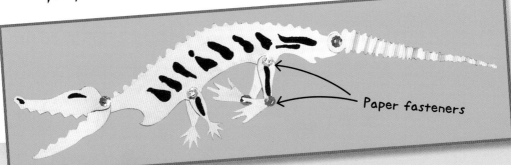

Paper fasteners

9

INVERTEBRATES

Invertebrates – animals without a backbone – have soft bodies. Some have a shell to protect them. Others have a skeleton on the outside of their body called an **exoskeleton**.

Exoskeletons

Arthropods are a group of animals with an exoskeleton. They include insects, spiders and centipedes. An exoskeleton is like a tough skin. It doesn't grow, so when an arthropod gets bigger, it sheds its exoskeleton and grows a new one.

Worms

Worms are also invertebrates. They do not have a skeleton. There are many different types of worm. Earthworms are found in flowerbeds and lawns. Their long, soft body is made up of **segments**.

Earthworms eat soil and dead plants. The waste they leave behind keeps the soil rich.

MAKE A WORMERY

Ask an adult to help you with this activity

You will need:
- **2-litre clear plastic bottle**
- **small clear plastic bottle**
- **scissors**
- **strong tape & sticky tape**
- **water**
- **trowel**
- **sand**
- **soil**
- **leaves**
- **thick black paper**
- **breadcrumbs**

1 Ask an adult to cut the top off the large bottle, and to cover the sharp edges with strong tape.

2 Fill the small bottle with water at room temperature. Replace the lid and put the small bottle inside the big bottle.

This will keep your worms visible against the sides of the big bottle.

3 Using the trowel, add a layer of sand to the space between the bottles about 3 cm deep. Add a layer of soil, then another of sand. Repeat until you have almost filled the big bottle. Put the leaves around the top of the soil. Add some water to make everything slightly damp.

4 Make a cylinder using black paper and sticky tape to cover the bottle loosely.

5 Find 3-4 big worms in a garden or park, and put them on top of the soil. Put the wormery in a cool place and keep the soil damp. Sprinkle breadcrumbs on the soil for food. Lift off the cylinder to watch the worms wriggling and tunnelling.

After a week, release the worms back where you found them.

REPRODUCTION

All animals can reproduce (make new life like themselves). This is essential to make sure animals do not become **extinct** and life on Earth can go on. New animal life begins with an egg.

Eggs

When an egg from a female animal is joined by a seed from a male, a new life begins and starts to grow. Most baby mammals grow inside their mother's body until they are ready to be born. Other animals lay eggs.

Life cycle

Animals go through a **life cycle**. They are born, they grow, they reproduce and die. Some animals change during this time. Butterflies, for example, start as an egg, which hatches into a caterpillar. The caterpillar becomes a **chrysalis** and changes into a butterfly.

Butterfly

The life cycle of a butterfly goes round and round, so life goes on.

Eggs

Chrysalis

Caterpillar

MAKE A BIRD BOX

A bird box in your garden can attract birds to nest and lay eggs there. Watch baby birds learn to feed themselves and fly. They may come back to the nest next spring to lay eggs and start a new life cycle.

Ask an adult to help you with this activity

You will need:

- **2-litre milk or juice carton, washed and dried**
- **scissors**
- **pen**
- **ruler**
- **waterproof glue**
- **hole punch**
- **string**

1 Ask an adult to help you cut off the top of the carton (including the spout) along the fold. Measure 12 cm up from the bottom of the carton and draw a line at this level all the way round. Cut from the open top down each edge as far as this line. Fold back the four flaps.

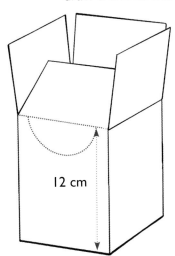

12 cm

2 Cut off one flap and cut a half-moon shape below it for birds to get in and out of the box. Fold the opposite flap down in half. Fold the side flaps across the top of the box and glue them together.

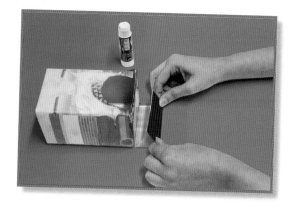

3 Punch a hole through the back folded flap, thread the string through and hang the box in a tree or hedge.

Keep a diary of the birds nesting in your box.

GROWING AND LEARNING

All animals grow from babies to adults. They need to learn essential skills to survive. Some animals learn from their parents. Others depend on **instincts** that tell them how to survive by themselves.

Baby deer learn to walk quickly so they can run from **predators**.

Learning and instinct

When baby ducklings hatch, they follow their mother into the water and learn to swim and feed themselves. Kittens fight and chase each other to learn to hunt. Other animals behave by instinct. They hatch and feed themselves without being taught these skills.

Growing up

Baby animals grow and learn at different rates. Elephants are fully grown at 15 years of age, while mice are fully grown at about 50 days. Human babies learn to walk at about one year old, but baby deer can walk as soon as they are born.

Ducklings learn to swim in their first few days of life.

COMPARE ANIMAL GROWTH RATES

You will need:
- **sheet of A3 paper**
- **ruler**
- **pens or crayons**
- **reference books**
- **computer**

1 Choose five animals of different sizes, such as an elephant, a deer, a human, a dog and a mouse. Draw a chart like the one below, but with wider columns for '1 year' and 'adult'.

2 Use books and the Internet to find information on how each animal grows.

At each stage, draw pictures of what they look like and write notes about what they can do.

Which animals develop the quickest?

Which develop the slowest?

	1 day		1 year	adult
Elephant		Dependent on mother. Mother helps newborn to stand to drink mother's milk.		
Deer		Dependent on mother. Learns to walk quickly to escape from predators.		
Human		Dependent on mother. Cries. Sleeps. Moves arms and legs. Drinks mother's milk.		
Dog		Dependent on mother. Blind. Deaf. No teeth. Sleeps. Crawls.		
Mouse		Dependent on mother. No fur. Blind. Drinks mother's milk.		

MOVEMENT

Most animals move around to find food and shelter and to escape from danger. They run, crawl, fly, swim and slither. Some animals, such as barnacles, find all they need in one place and stay there all their lives.

Sliding and slithering

Animals with no legs slide and slither over the ground. Snails and slugs have a long body with muscles that ripple and move them along. Snakes have hundreds of bones in their spine so they can coil and bend.

Anemones attach themselves to rocks in the sea. They mostly stay in one place.

Wings

Birds and insects have wings to fly around. Birds are the only animals with feathers. Wing feathers help to lift the bird up into the air when it flaps its wings to fly. Many insects beat their wings so fast that they vibrate and make a buzzing sound.

Sea birds use their wings to glide over water, looking for fish to eat.

MAKE A SEAGULL THAT FLAPS ITS WINGS

Ask an adult to help you with this activity

You will need:
- **sheet of A4 white card**
- **sheet of thick A4 paper**
- **pencil**
- **scissors**
- **25 cm dowel (thin rod of wood)**
- **sticky tape**
- **thin string**
- **needle**
- **bead**

1 Copy the templates of the seagull's body, the tab and the tail onto the card. Copy the seagull's wings onto the paper. Cut out the shapes.

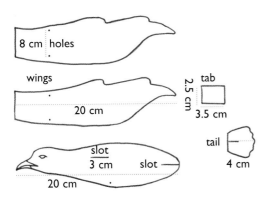

2 Ask an adult to help you make small holes and slots in the seagull's wings and body, where shown. Cut two lengths of string 60 cm long, and one 30 cm long.

3 Push the tab through the slot in the middle of the seagull's body and fix it with sticky tape. Push the tail through the slot at the end of the body. Stick the wings to the tab with sticky tape so the edges line up exactly, but don't overlap.

4 Thread the long strings through the holes on each wing and tie with a knot. Thread the shorter length through the hole at the bottom of the body, thread on the bead and tie a loop.

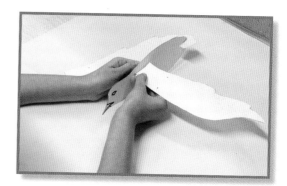

5 Loop the wing strings over the dowel. Pull down gently on the bead and then let go, to watch your seagull flap its wings.

FOOD AND EATING

Plants and animals depend on each other to survive. We need to look after them for life on Earth to continue. If one plant or animal dies out, it can affect other plants and animals, too.

Food chains

A **food chain** describes the way animals and plants are linked by what they eat. For example, barn owls eat voles, which in turn eat insects and plants. If the plants are cut down, the voles may die out, and the barn owls will lose part of their diet.

Barn owls are rarely hunted. They are found at the top of a food chain.

Teeth

Animals can be divided into three groups – meat eaters called carnivores, plant eaters called herbivores and plant and meat eaters called omnivores. Omnivores have different-shaped teeth to tear and grind their food. Birds have no teeth at all.

A tiger is a carnivore. It has sharp, pointed teeth to tear through meat.

MATCH THE TEETH!

Match herbivores, carnivores and omnivores to their teeth.

You will need:
- **white card**
- **pencils and crayons**
- **scissors**

1 Cut the card into 18 playing card-sized rectangles. Using the table below as a guide, make six sets of three cards. Draw a picture or write a word on each card to show an animal, its teeth, and the group it belongs to – carnivore, omnivore or herbivore. Play the game with a friend. The first to collect two sets of three cards that go together is the winner!

2 Deal four cards each and place the remaining cards face down in a pile. Pick up one card from the pile, without showing it to your friend. Put a card you don't want face down, starting a new pile of cards.

3 Ask your friend to pick up a card from the first pile and to put down a card on the second pile. When the first pile of cards has been used, start to use the second pile. Try to keep cards that will make up a set.

4 As soon as one player has a set, lay them out and pick three more cards off the pile. Carry on until one player gets two complete sets and wins!

Picture	Picture	Word
Lion		Carnivore
Shark		Carnivore
Human		Omnivore
Gorilla		Omnivore
Sheep		Herbivore
Cow		Herbivore

ANIMAL SENSES

Animals sense the world around them through seeing, hearing, touching, smelling and tasting. Their senses are **adapted** to their own needs. For example, hawks have very good eyesight for hunting, but moles living underground can see very little.

A snake's forked tongue collects scents in the air.

Sense organs

Some animals have sense organs that are different from ours. Whiskers, for example, are long, thick hairs that grow around the nose and mouth of some animals, such as dogs and mice. They sense nearby objects and movements. Insects have long **antennae** they can move around to feel, smell and taste. Snakes flick their forked tongues to smell and taste the air.

Bees fly from flower to flower. They use their antennae to touch, taste and smell.

Sight and hearing

Animals have adapted their senses of sight and hearing to hunt, or to escape from danger. Rabbits can swivel their large ears to hear the smallest sound that might be a predator. Wolves run over long distances looking for **prey**. They can see straight ahead and to each side because their eyes are set wide apart on their heads.

Rabbits move their large ears to listen for danger.

ACTIVITY

HOW FAR IS IT?

Find out how two eyes help you to work out distance accurately.

You will need:
- **pen with a lid**
- **small ball**

1 With the pen in one hand and the lid in the other, hold your hands out in front of you. Put the lid on the pen. Now try with one eye shut. Is it more difficult?

2 Count how many tries it takes before you adapt to using one eye and can put the lid straight on the pen.

3 Now try catching a ball. Shut one eye and do it again. How long does it take to become good at catching a ball with one eye shut? Can you catch the ball with just one hand?

Because you are used to judging distance using both eyes, it will take a few tries to work out distance accurately with one eye closed. What other activities do you do that need the help of both eyes?

PETS

Pets are animals we keep at home. Animals living in the wild look after themselves. Pet owners have to feed their pets, keep them clean, make sure they have enough exercise and take them to the vet if they are ill.

Hutches and cages

Small pets, such as hamsters, are kept in cages. Rabbits and guinea pigs are kept in hutches. Hutches and cages should be kept clean with fresh straw or sawdust. They need to be big enough for the animals to run around, hide and build a nest.

Cats and dogs

Two of the most common pets are cats and dogs. They can be trained to live with people and to follow simple instructions. Dogs obey words such as 'sit', 'down' and 'heel'. Cats learn to sleep in a cat basket. Dogs and cats give their owners friendship and fun.

A hamster can run on a wheel for extra exercise.

Taking your dog for a walk is good exercise with family and friends!

MAKE A PLAYGROUND FOR SMALL PETS

You will need:

- **large cardboard box with high sides**
- **wooden ruler**
- **wooden blocks**
- **cardboard tube**
- **ping-pong ball (or other pet toys)**

1 Make a see-saw by balancing a wooden ruler across a wooden block inside the cardboard box.

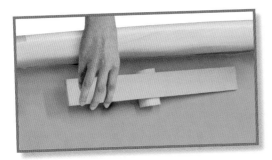

2 Arrange the wooden blocks to make a maze. Pile them up in the shape of steps – but not near the sides of the box!

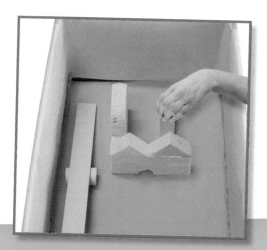

3 Tape the cardboard tube to the base of the box, or to some of the bricks, to make a tunnel for your pet to run through.

4 Put in the ping-pong ball, a bell or other pet toys. Use your imagination to make an exciting playground for your pet, but make sure it can't hurt itself on the equipment.

Keep watch while your pet is playing so it doesn't chew a hole in the box or escape over the sides!

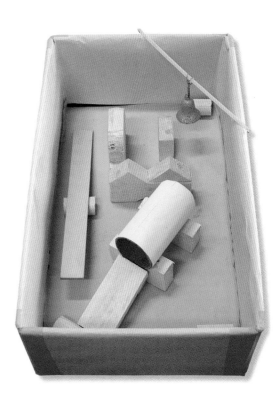

ADAPTATION

Animals adapt over millions of years to survive in their habitats. Polar bears, for example, have thick, white fur to protect them in the Arctic snow. Some animals have to move to different habitats in order to survive.

Camouflage

Some animals adapt using **camouflage** to stay hidden. A tiger's stripy coat blends in with long grasses so it can creep up on its prey. A chameleon changes colour as it moves between green and brown leaves and branches, and stays very still to fool predators.

A herd of wildebeest graze grass in one area and then move on.

This chameleon has changed colour to make it difficult to find among its new surroundings.

Migration

Many animals **migrate** to find the best supply of food and water. Herds of wildebeest, for example, travel over a thousand kilometres each year searching for water and grass to eat. When supplies run out, the wildebeest are forced to look elsewhere.

MAKE A SURVEY OF LOCAL ANIMAL COLOURS

You will need:
- **camera or coloured pencils and paper**

1 Look for small animals, such as birds and insects, around your school or where you live. Look among piles of leaves, under stones, in the soil, on plants and among leaves and branches. How many different animals can you find? Where did you find most animals?

2 Take a photograph or draw a picture. Copy the colours of the animal and its surroundings carefully.

3 Write notes on why you think the animal is a particular colour. For example:

> **This brown, speckled sparrow is pecking for food under the hedge. It is hard to spot because it is the same colour as its background. It can eat undisturbed.**

4 Organise your pictures in two columns – animals that are easy to spot, and animals that are hard to spot.

Easy to spot	Hard to spot
Butterfly	Caterpillar
Ladybird	Earthworm
Magpie	Earwig

CARING FOR ANIMALS

Animals need to be cared for whether they are pets or live in the wild. People can harm wild animals by hunting them or by destroying their habitats. There are things we can all do to help care for animals.

The environment

All living things need a healthy, clean **environment** to survive. Keeping the environment free of litter is one way we can protect animals. Some animals eat (or become trapped in) old plastic bags, for example. Another serious threat to animals is **global warming**, which is changing natural habitats. Recycling materials and using less fuel are some of the things we can do to reduce global warming.

Using reusable shopping bags can help to reduce the number of plastic bags that litter the environment.

As the sea warms and the ice melts, it becomes more difficult for penguins and polar bears to find their food.

Species at risk

Animals are at great risk when their habitats are destroyed. They lose their homes and there is less food to go around. When trees are cut down for wood or to create farmland, or when seas and oceans become polluted, many animals are put in danger.

Ocean creatures are at risk from polluted seas and warming waters.

ACTIVITY

HELP PROTECT A LOCAL WILDLIFE HABITAT

1 Look in a local newspaper or use the Internet to find out where there is a wildlife habitat in danger near to your home or school. It could be a pond choked with weeds, a beach or stream full of litter, a meadow that is going to be built on, or a wood or a tree that is due to be cut down.

3 You could join a group to help clean-up the habitat or campaign to save it. Remember that ponds, beaches, streams and rivers can be dangerous. Always have an adult with you if you visit these places.

2 Find out what animals live there and make a list. Find out all you can about each animal and the importance of its habitat.

These children are helping to clean a river bank to save the habitat for local wildlife.

Glossary

adapted

Something that has adapted has changed over time to survive.

antennae

Antennae are feelers that some animals use to sense their surroundings.

arthropod

An arthropod belongs to a group of animals that have an exoskeleton.

camouflage

Camouflage is the way animals use colour and patterns to blend in with their surroundings.

characteristics

Characteristics are qualities that help us to recognise things. For example, a characteristic of humans is that they move around.

chrysalis

A chrysalis is a stage some insects go through in their life cycle. A caterpillar becomes a chrysalis.

environment

The environment is the surroundings in which animals and plants live.

exoskeleton

An exoskeleton is a hard, protective covering on the outside of animals with soft bodies. Insects, for example, have a tough exoskeleton.

extinct

Animals or plants that are extinct have died out completely.

food chain

A food chain is the way animals are linked together, like links in a chain, by what they eat.

gills

Gills are an organ that fish and some amphibians use to extract oxygen from water.

global warming

Global warming is the rise in the Earth's temperature. It is partly caused by burning fuels such as gas and oil.

habitat

A habitat is the natural environment of a plant or animal. For example, the ocean is the habitat of dolphins.

instincts

Instincts are natural kinds of behaviour that help animals to survive.

kingdom

Natural things are divided into five groups or kingdoms, the largest of which are the animal and plant kingdoms.

life cycle

A life cycle describes the way life goes round and round like a circle. Animals are born, they grow, they make new life like themselves so life can go on, and they die.

mammals

Mammals are a group of animals that have warm blood and hair on their body. Baby mammals drink their mother's milk.

migrate

To migrate is to travel long distances to find food and water.

predator

A predator is an animal that hunts and kills other animals for food.

prey

Prey are animals that are hunted by other animals for food.

reproduce

Animals and plants reproduce to make new life like themselves.

segment

A segment is a part of something. The body of an insect is divided into three segments or parts.

skeleton

A skeleton is a frame made up of bones. It gives animals their shape, supports them and protects soft body parts such as the brain.

species

A species is a group of animals or plants that are similar to each other. A dog is a species of animal and seaweed is a species of plant.

Quiz

1 How many different types of animals belong to the animal kingdom?

a) about two hundred
b) about two thousand
c) about twenty thousand
d) about two million

2 What do animals breathe in?

a) oxygen
b) carbon dioxide
c) nitrogen
d) helium

3 Humans belong to which animal group?

a) amphibians
b) mammals
c) reptiles
d) insects

4 Which animal is NOT an invertebrate?

a) spider
b) worm
c) snake
d) snail

5 Put these stages of the butterfly life cycle in the correct order.

a) butterfly
b) caterpillar
c) chrysalis
d) eggs

6 Elephants are fully grown at:

a) 2 years of age
b) 5 years of age
c) 10 years of age
d) 15 years of age

7 Birds are the only animals that have:

a) wings
b) feathers
c) webbed feet
d) claws

8 What do omnivores eat?

a) meat and plants
b) meat only
c) plants only
d) nothing

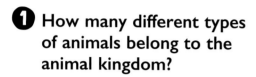

9 Bees use their antennae to:

a) touch, taste and hear
b) touch, smell and hear
c) touch, taste and smell
d) touch, taste and see

10 Animals adapt to suit their surroundings. This takes place over:

a) millions of years
b) thousands of years
c) hundreds of years
d) about ten years

ANSWERS 1d, 2a, 3b, 4c, 5a/d/b/c, 6d, 7b, 8a, 9c, 10a

FURTHER INFORMATION

BOOKS

Body Bits: Astounding Animal Body Facts by Paul Mason, Wayland

Extreme Science: Incredible Living Things by Jon Richards, Wayland

A Question of Science: Why can't penguins fly? by Anna Claybourne, Wayland

Endangered Wildlife by Anita Ganeri, Wayland

WEBSITES

All about animal classification www.bbc.co.uk/bitesize/topics/zn22pv4

Video clips of animals in action www.bbc.co.uk/bitesize/topics/zn22pv4/resources/1

Top facts about your favourite animals www.natgeokids.com/uk/category/discover/animals

Learn about animal species at risk www.worldwildlife.org/species

Index

Titles in the DISCOVER AND DO! SCIENCE series

- What are animals?
- Vertebrates
- Invertebrates
- Reproduction
- Growing and learning
- Movement
- Food and eating
- Animal senses
- Pets
- Adaptation
- Caring for animals

- What is electricity?
- Natural electricity
- Batteries
- Current and circuits
- Circuits and switches
- Circuit symbols
- What are conductors?
- Making electricity
- Using electricity
- Saving electricity
- Keeping safe

- What are forces?
- Pushes and pulls
- Moving
- Gravity and weight
- Floating and sinking
- Friction
- Drag
- Elasticity
- Magnetism
- Using forces
- Wind and water

- Your body
- A healthy body
- Brain and nerves
- Heart and circulation
- Breathing
- Skeleton and bones
- Muscles and movement
- Digestion
- Skin
- Senses
- Life cycle

- What is light?
- What is dark?
- Light rays
- Shadows
- Shining through
- Reflection
- Refraction
- Bigger and smaller
- Different kinds of light
- Seeing and light
- Coloured light

- What are materials?
- What is a solid?
- What is a liquid?
- What is a gas?
- Water
- Mixtures and solutions
- Heat
- Melt and mould
- Squash and stretch
- Recycling materials
- Modern materials

- What is a plant?
- Parts of a plant
- What do plants need?
- Making food
- Flowers
- Germination
- Bulbs and tubers
- Spreading seeds
- Plant adaptation
- Plants for life
- Caring for plants

- Sounds around us
- Vibrations
- Moving sound
- Making sounds
- Hearing sounds
- Animal hearing
- Near and far
- Bouncing sound
- Musical sounds
- Changing sounds
- Ultrasound

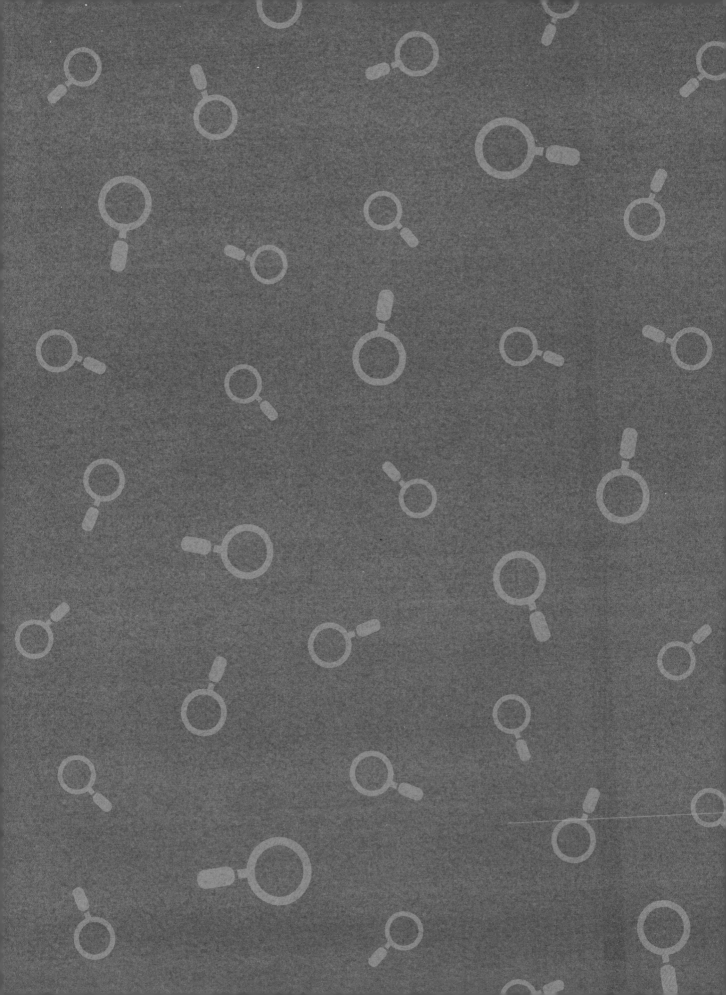